How Do Dinosaurs Eat Their Food?

W9-AHJ-244

DEINONYCHUS

PROTOCERATOPS

LAMBEOSAURUS

POLACANTHUS

AMARGASAURUS

GORGOSAURUS

CRYOLOPHOSAURUS

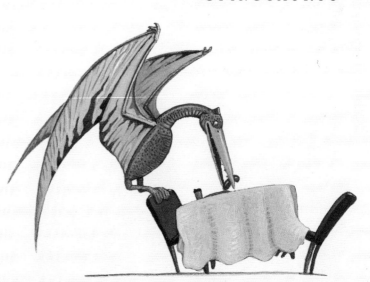

SPINOSAURUS

SUPERSAURUS

QUETZALCOATLUS

DEINONYCHUS

PROTOCERATOPS

LAMBEOSAURUS

POLACANTHUS

AMARGASAURUS

CRYOLOPHOSAURUS

GORGOSAURUS

SPINOSAURUS

SUPERSAURUS

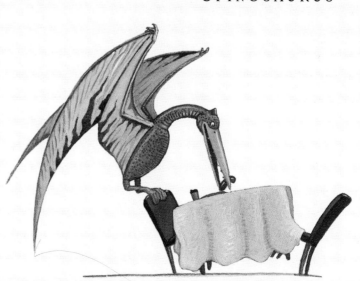

QUETZALCOATLUS

JANE YOLEN

How Do Dinosaurs Eat Their Food?

Eat Their Food?

Illustrated by

MARK TEAGUE

SCHOLASTIC INC.
New York Toronto London Auckland Sydney
Mexico City New Delhi Hong Kong Buenos Aires

No part of this publication may be reproduced, stored in a retrieval system,
or transmitted in any form or by any means, electronic, mechanical, photocopying,
recording, or otherwise, without written permission of the publisher. For information
regarding permission, write to Scholastic Inc., Attention:
Permissions Department, 557 Broadway, New York, NY 10012.

This book was originally published in hardcover by the Blue Sky Press in 2005.

ISBN-13: 978-0-439-24103-8
ISBN-10: 0-439-24103-0

Text copyright © 2005 by Jane Yolen.

Illustrations copyright © 2005 by Mark Teague.

All rights reserved. Published by Scholastic Inc. SCHOLASTIC and associated
logos are trademarks and/or registered trademarks of Scholastic Inc.

12 11 10 9 8 7 6 5 4 3 2 1   6 7 8 9 10 11/0

Printed in the U.S.A.   08

First Scholastic paperback printing, September 2006

To wee David, who is a splendid dinosaur

J. Y.

For Michael Cavanaugh

M. T.

How does a dinosaur
eat all his food?
Does he burp,
does he belch,
or make noises
quite rude?

Does he pick at his cereal,
throw down

his cup,

Does he fuss, does he fidget,
or squirm in his chair?

Does he flip his spaghetti high into the air?

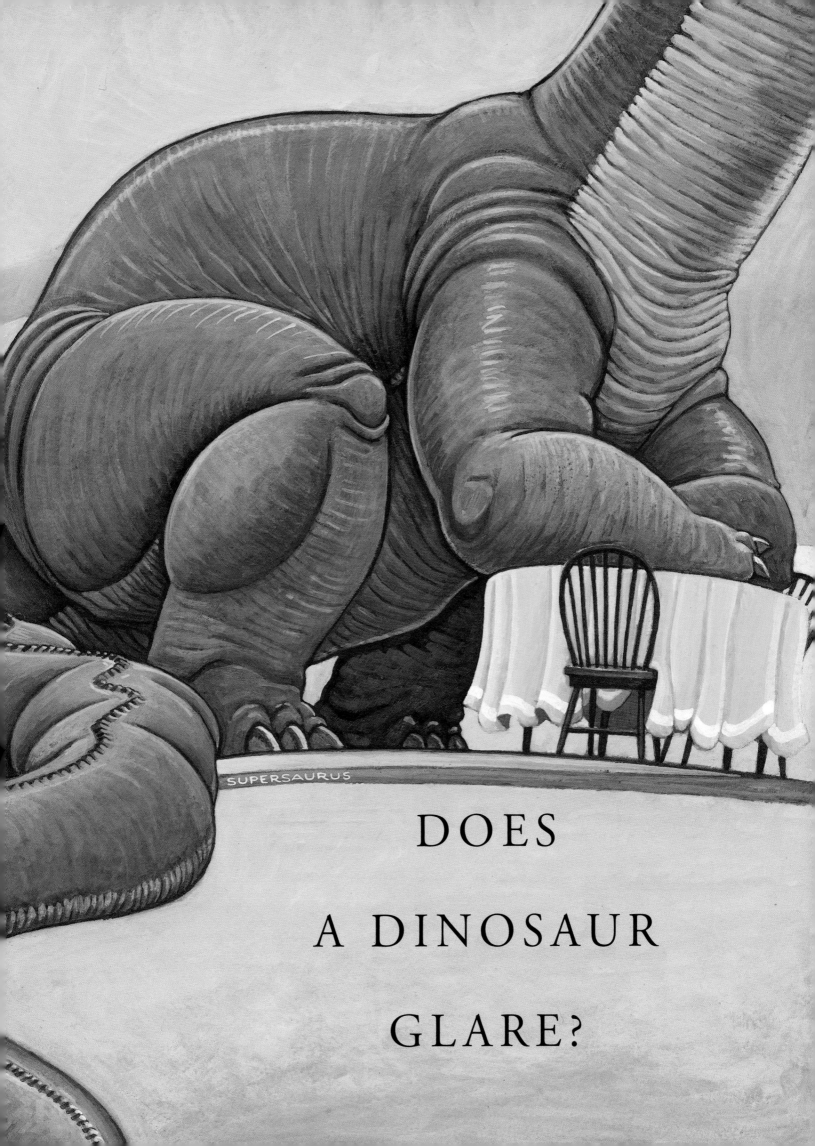

DOES

A DINOSAUR

GLARE?

How does a dinosaur
eat all his food?

Does he spit
out his broccoli
partially chewed?

SPINOSAURUS

Does he bubble

his milk?

Stick beans

up his nose?

GORGOSAURUS

Does he squeeze juicy oranges

with his big toes?

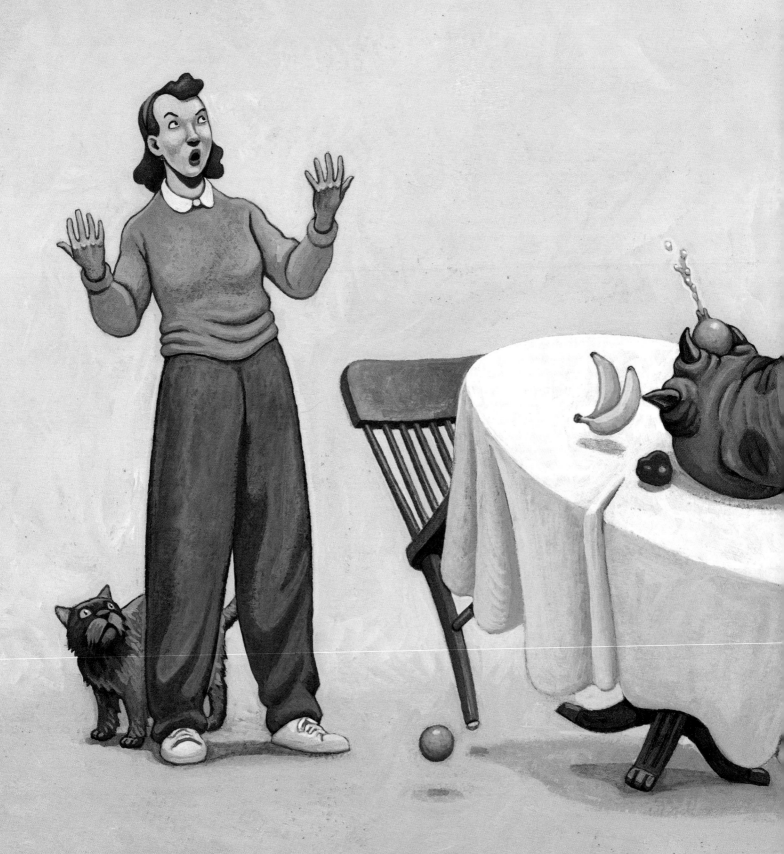

No . . .

He says, "Please"

and "Thank you."
He sits very still.

He eats all before him
with smiles and goodwill.

He tries
every new thing,
at least one
small bite.

He makes

no loud noises—

that isn't polite.

He never
drops anything
onto the floor.
And after
he's finished,
he asks for
some more.

Eat up.

Eat up, little dinosaur.

DEINONYCHUS

PROTOCERATOPS

LAMBEOSAURUS

POLACANTHUS

AMARGASAURUS

GORGOSAURUS

CRYOLOPHOSAURUS

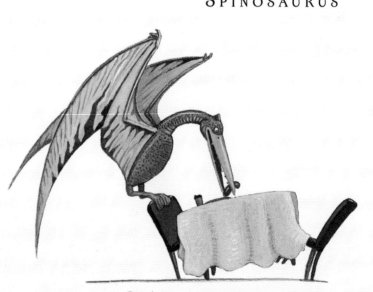

SPINOSAURUS

SUPERSAURUS

QUETZALCOATLUS

DEINONYCHUS

PROTOCERATOPS

LAMBEOSAURUS

POLACANTHUS

CRYOLOPHOSAURUS

AMARGASAURUS

GORGOSAURUS

SPINOSAURUS

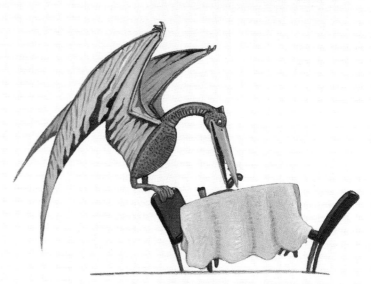

SUPERSAURUS

QUETZALCOATLUS